THE MAHABHARATA
CHILDREN'S ILLUSTRATED CLASSICS

The GREAT ESCAPE

Retold by **CHARU AGARWAL DHANDIA**
Art **KAVITA SINGH KALE** Design **RACHITA RAKYAN**

Published by
Rupa Publications India Pvt. Ltd 2020
7/16, Ansari Road, Daryaganj
New Delhi 110002

Sales centres:
Allahabad Bengaluru Chennai
Hyderabad Jaipur Kathmandu
Kolkata Mumbai

Edition copyright © Rupa Publications Pvt. Ltd 2020

All rights reserved.
No part of this publication may be reproduced, transmitted,
or stored in a retrieval system, in any form or by any means, electronic, mechanical, photocopying,
recording or otherwise,
without the prior permission of the publisher.

ISBN: 978-81-291-4972-5

First impression 2020

10 9 8 7 6 5 4 3 2 1

The moral right of the author has been asserted.

Printed at Nutech Print Services - India

This book is sold subject to the condition that it shall not, by way of trade or otherwise, be lent,
resold, hired out, or otherwise circulated, without the publisher's prior consent, in any form of
binding or cover other than that in which it is published.

Charu Agarwal Dhandia weaves together her two biggest passions—studying Indian classical literature and creative storytelling. She is an economist by training and works in the social development space.

Kavita Singh Kale's background as an artist and a designer enables her to draw a thin line between design following functionality and pure self-expression. This has helped her evolve as a transmedia artist. Her work includes art installations, children's books, comics, paintings and videos.

Rachita Rakyan combines over 15 years of expertise in graphic design and art direction with deep understanding of functionality and aesthetics across print, publishing, branding and digital media.

CONTENTS

KURU DYNASTY	*IV-V*
KEY CHARACTERS	*VI-VII*
THE TRAP AT VARANASI	1
THE SECRET TUNNEL	13
THE ESCAPE	20
THE NEWS OF THE ACCIDENT	27
PANDAVAS IN EKACHARYA	33
BHIMA FACES BAKASURA	45

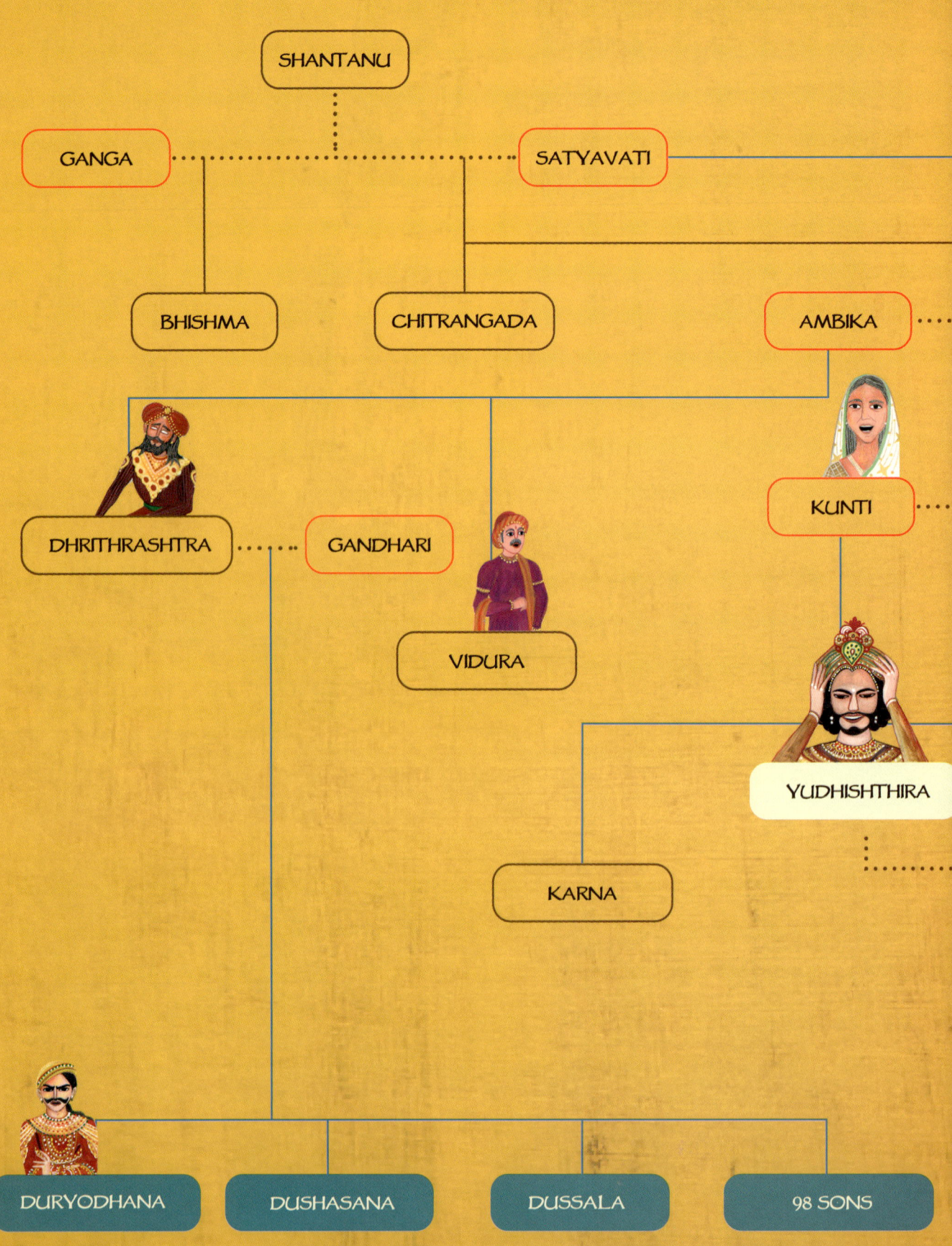

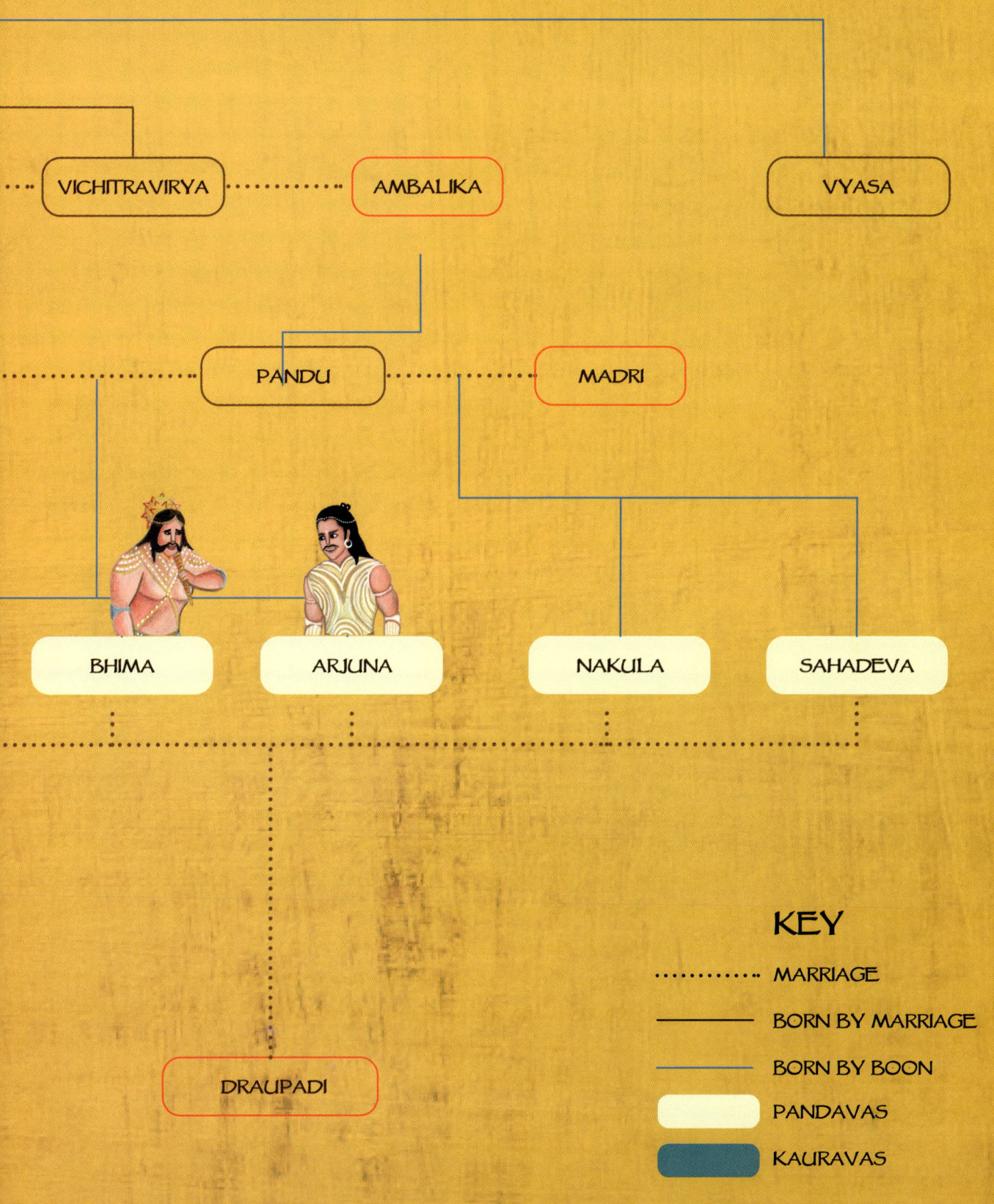

KEY CHARACTERS

KUNTI

Kunti, the daughter of King Kuntibhoja, was blessed by sage Durvasa for taking care of him. He gave her a magic chant that she could use to make any god appear and give her a son. Using this chant when she was very young, she got Karna, a son from the sun god, Surya. Later five Pandava brothers were born with the help of the chant.

VIDURA

Vidura was born by the boon of sage Vyasa to the maid of princess Ambika. He was a wise man with a kind heart and served as the minister in the court of his half-brothers, Pandu and Dhrithrashtra. Vidura was greatly fond of the Pandavas, who often turned to him for advice.

YUDHISHTHIRA

Yudhishthira was the eldest Pandava, born to Kunti as a blessing from Lord Dharma. He ruled Indraprastha and later Hastinapur. Yudhishthira proved to be a great ruler and was known for his virtues of honesty, loyalty, justice, tolerance and brotherhood.

DURYODHANA

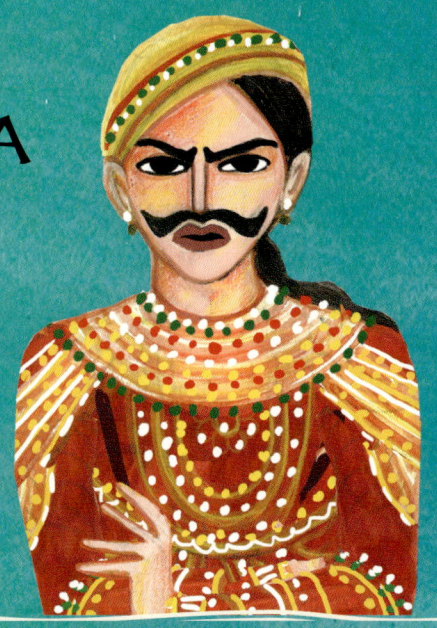

Duryodhana was the eldest brother amongst the Kauravas and born to princess Gandhari as a blessing from sage Vyasa. He was very jealous of the Pandavas.

BHIMA

Bhima was the second of the Pandavas, born to Kunti. He was immensely strong and protected his family from every danger. He married Hidimbi and later Draupadi.

BAKASURA

Bakasura was a giant living on a hilltop in Ekacharya. The people of Ekacharya had to send enormous amounts of food along with one family member for him to eat. Bhima fought Bakasura and defeated him.

THE TRAP AT VARANASI

Yudhishthira was the eldest of the Pandavas and the ruler of Hastinapur. He was a brave king and was loved by the people of Hastinapur. The Pandava brothers soon became very popular.

Duryodhana, the eldest Kaurava prince, and his uncle Shakuni were jealous of the growing popularity of the Pandavas. Duryodhana's jealousy had turned him evil.

Duryodhana convinced his father Dhrithrashtra to send the Pandavas to the Shiva festival at Varanasi. He and his uncle Shakuni had made a plan to harm the Pandavas at the festival.

One morning, he and Shakuni called for Purochana, a minister. Purochana bowed in respect and asked, 'What can I do for you, My Lord?'

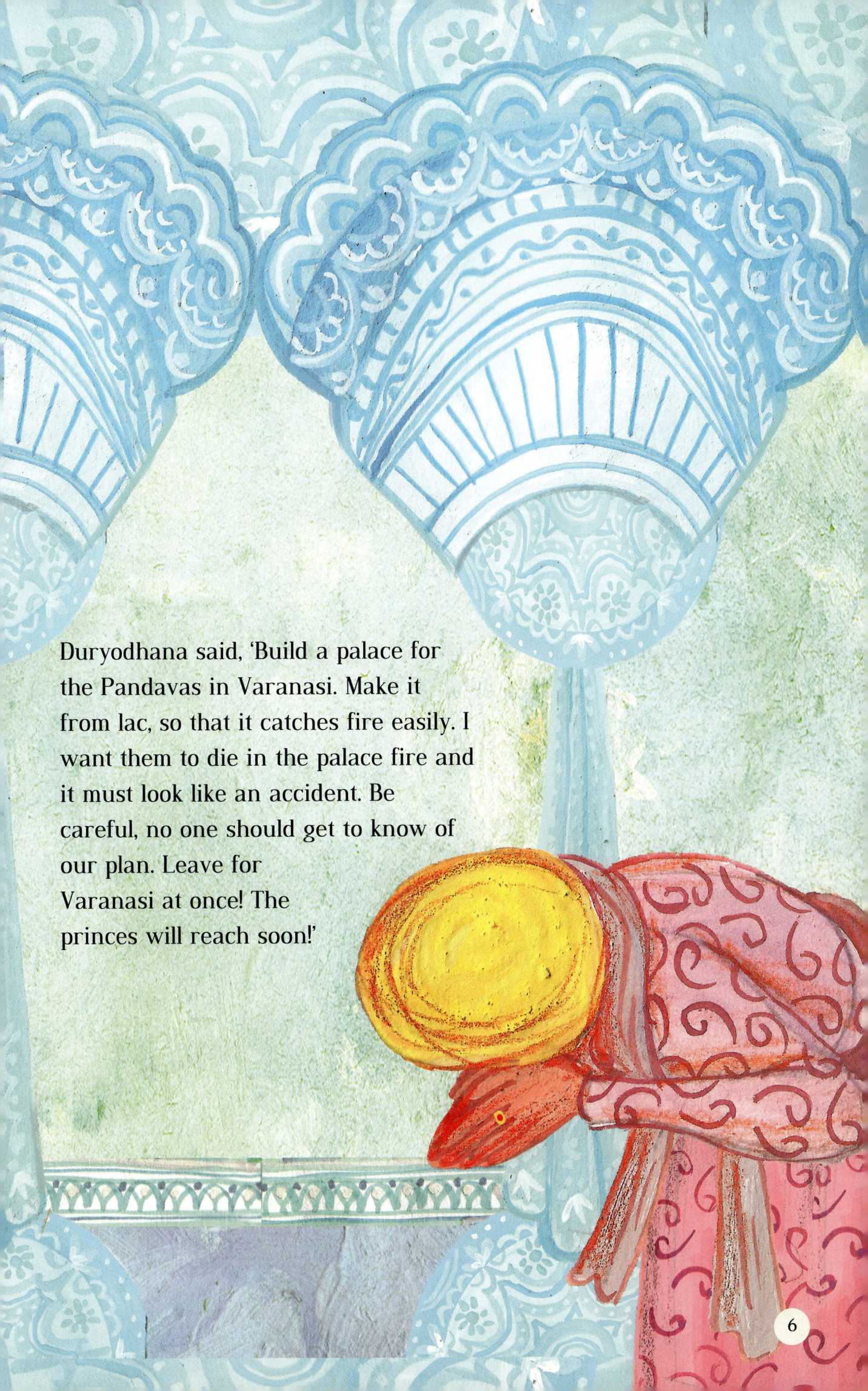

Duryodhana said, 'Build a palace for the Pandavas in Varanasi. Make it from lac, so that it catches fire easily. I want them to die in the palace fire and it must look like an accident. Be careful, no one should get to know of our plan. Leave for Varanasi at once! The princes will reach soon!'

Vidura, the minister, was a kind-hearted man and very fond of the Pandavas. He overheard the conversation between Duryodhana and Purochana about the lac palace.

Vidura was worried. He wanted to save the Pandavas and wondered how he could warn them of Duryodhana's evil plan.

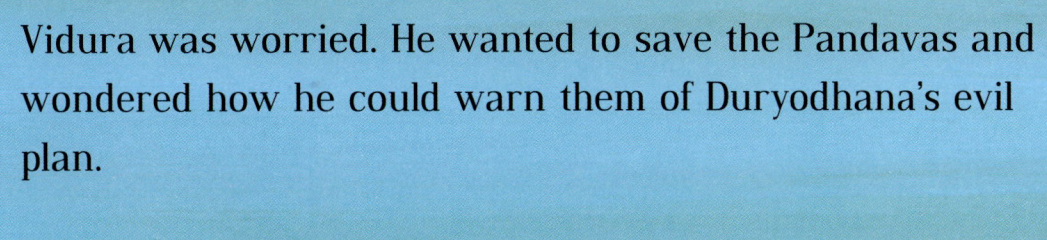

When the Pandavas were leaving Hastinapur, Vidura rushed to Yudhishthira and pulled him to a corner. He whispered in Yudhishthira's ear, 'There is danger in Varanasi. Stay safe from fire. You must protect your brothers and mother from fire. Remember this.'

But Yudhishthira did not understand what Vidura meant.

He simply nodded and got on the chariot with his brothers and Kunti. They waved goodbye to all the people who had gathered, and left for the festival at Varanasi.

THE SECRET TUNNEL

The grand Shiva festival started with great enthusiasm. There were celebrations all around with an elaborate spread of games, food and shops selling many things.

Purochana led the Pandavas to the lac palace. The princes followed him, unaware of the danger Duryodhana had planned for them.

The moment the princes entered the palace gates, they could smell something strange. Yudhishthira signalled the others to wait at the gates while he went inside to inspect the palace. In a short while, he returned to his brothers and said, 'The palace is made of lac and other inflammable materials. Now I understand why Vidura warned me of fire! Duryodhana has laid a trap for us here!'

The Pandavas looked at each other, scared and angry. Yudhishthira continued, 'We cannot let Purochana know that we have found out their secret plan. We have to be very careful or we can get into further trouble.'

The brothers sat up all night trying to figure out a plan to escape the palace secretly. They did not want anybody to know that they had escaped safely.

THE ESCAPE

Back in Hastinapur, Vidura was getting anxious. What would happen to the Pandavas in Varanasi? He paced from end to end in his chambers, thinking of a way to save the princes.

Finally, he came up with a plan. He asked his minister to bring the local mason to him.

The mason entered Vidura's chambers and bowed. Vidura said, 'I want you to dig a secret passage leading out of the palace of the Pandavas in Varanasi. The passage must lead them to the forest. You have one night to complete the job. And remember, no one must get to know about the secret tunnel.'

The next morning, the mason reached the lac palace and informed the Pandavas of Vidura's plan. All night, he dug a secret passage leading into the forest. The Pandavas had planned to escape the next day.

When they came back from the festival, Yudhishthira whispered, 'Bhima, we must now set the palace on fire. It is time for us to escape!'

Bhima nodded and lit a matchstick. At once, the palace walls caught fire. Quickly they rushed to the secret tunnel. First they helped their mother escape and then followed, one by one. Soon they found themselves safe outside a forest on the banks of river Yamuna.
They turned back to look at the blazing lac palace far away.
Silently, they thanked Vidura for saving their lives.

THE NEWS OF THE ACCIDENT

The news of the accident reached far and wide. People in Varanasi gathered in huge crowds, in grief. The news soon reached Hastinapur. Duryodhana and Shakuni were joyous at the success of their plan but pretended to be sad and in shock.

Bhishma, the great grandfather of the Pandavas, loved them dearly. He was deeply saddened at the news of their accident. He rushed to Varanasi along with Dhrithrashtra, Duryodhana and Vidura.

On seeing Bhishma so sad, Vidura leaned towards him and said, 'Don't worry, the Pandavas are safe. I have made sure they escaped from the palace.'

Bhishma's face lit up. He sighed in relief and looked at Vidura with gratitude.

The Pandavas, in the meantime, had crossed the river and reached a thick forest.

PANDAVAS IN EKACHARYA

After walking for some time, the Pandavas reached a quiet town called Ekacharya. They looked for a place to stay. Soon they reached the house of a Brahmin family. The family welcomed them generously.

They welcomed Kunti and the Pandavas into their house. The Pandavas disguised themselves as brahmins and began living with the brahmin family.

Every morning, the princes would go to the village to earn money and food. In the evening, their mother would divide their earnings equally among the brothers.

One afternoon, Bhima and Kunti were alone at home.

Suddenly they heard loud sobbing sounds coming from the far end of the house.

Kunti said to Bhima, 'Son, I think the brahmin family is in trouble. They gave us shelter when we needed it. It is now our duty to help them in their troubles!'

Kunti went over to the side of the house where the householders were sitting. She asked, 'What is the matter?'

The old brahmin raised his head and said, 'Our village is facing a big problem. A giant called Bakasura lives in a nearby cave. Every month, a household sends a family member along with enormous amounts of food, to feed him. Today, it is our family's turn.'
The man started weeping.

Kunti shook her head and said, 'Don't worry, you will not have to send anyone to the giant. My son Bhima is stronger than everyone else. He will defeat Bakasura!'

'How can I let that happen? You are our guests. We cannot let Bakasura harm our guest,' the brahmin said worriedly. Kunti said, 'Bhima is very brave. He will fight Bakasura and protect the entire village.'

Kunti returned to her sons. The brothers sat down for dinner after the day's work. She sat beside them to narrate the story of Bakasura. Bhima listened to his mother obediently. He said, 'You are right, Mother. The village needs my help. I will fight Bakasura.'

BHIMA FACES BAKASURA

45

The next morning, Bhima sat in the food cart meant for Bakasura and left the brahmin's house.

On reaching the top of the hill, Bhima opened the food packets and started eating. He let out a loud grunt to attract Bakasura's attention.

Bakasura heard Bhima and rushed to the hilltop. He was shocked to see Bhima sitting and eating the food brought for him.

It made Bakasura furious! He opened his wide mouth and roared, 'HOW DARE YOU EAT MY FOOD? DO YOU WANT TO BE EATEN AS WELL?'

Saying this, Bakasura leapt on Bhima. But before Bakasura could touch him, Bhima sprang up and pushed the giant with his strong arms. Bakasura fell on the ground.

Bakasura clenched his fists and got up. They grappled for sometime till Bhima defeated the giant Bakasura.

The news of Bakasura's death reached Ekacharya. There were celebrations all around.

Thanks to Bhima, the people of Ekacharya were finally free from the mighty giant Bakasura and lived happily, without fear.

TITLES IN THIS SERIES

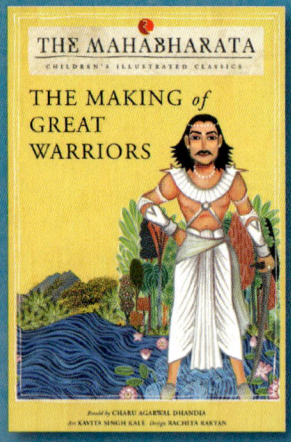
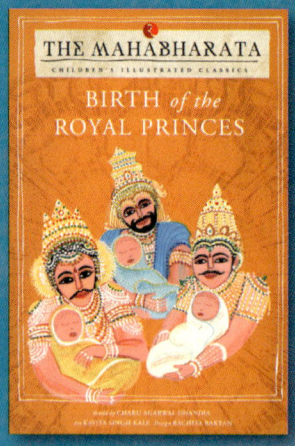
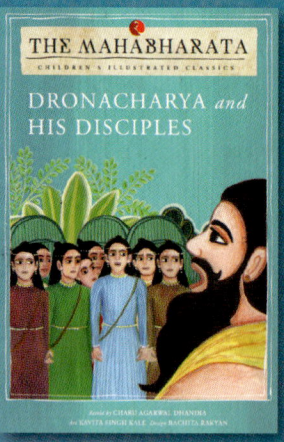
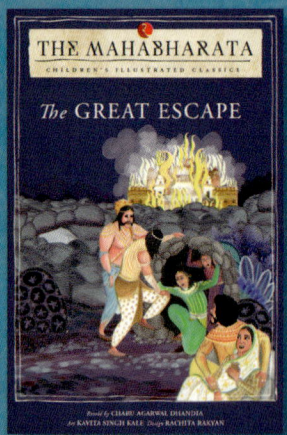
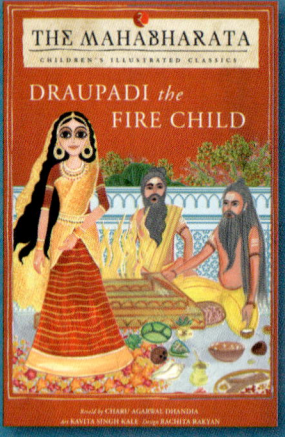
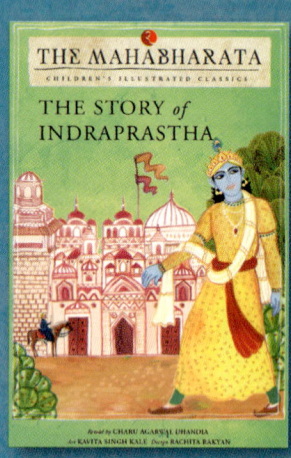
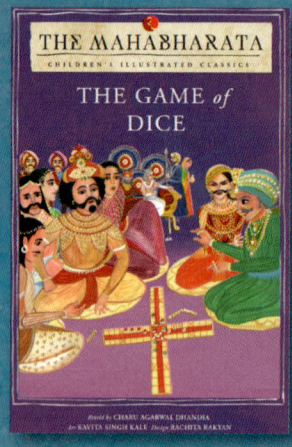
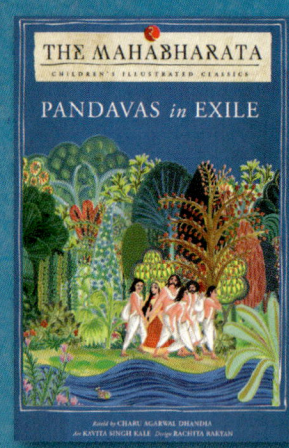
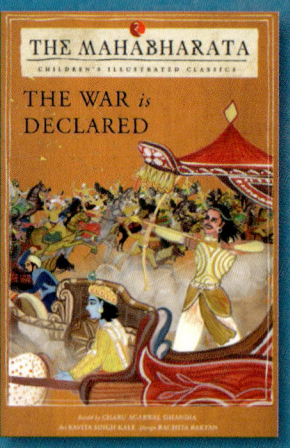